THE ADVENTURES OF
TRICKEY, ICKEY, SLICKEY AND THE BAD CAT EARL: THE BEGINNING

Charles F. McClure

THE ADVENTURES OF
TRICKEY, ICKEY, SLICKEY AND THE BAD CAT EARL: THE BEGINNING

This book is dedicated to Jameson Staton

ReadersMagnet, LLC

THE ADVENTURES OF TRICKEY, ICKEY, SLICKEY AND THE BAD CAT EARL: THE BEGINNING

This story started because three mice Trickey, Ickey and Slickey never let a cat named Earl out smart them. Earl wasn't stupid but the mice were very smart and had plenty of help from their friends and some really dumb friends of Earls.

They all lived on a farm in the remote part of up state New York. Most people don't think of corn fields when they think of New York. but in the out lying areas they do grow corn and other veggies. Which in the summer made for plenty of food for every one, animals included. There were also beautiful meadows full of grasses and flowers.

One day in mid May farmer Bob was tilling a field on a warm day, the mice thought they would go for a walk around the farm, unbeknown to them Earl the cat was watching their every move, he wanted to catch them alone and eat them. But that was not as easy as he thought it would be.

Earl was a very sneaky cat and would have caught them already if it had not been for all them little pesky farm animals who thought the world of the mice and didn't much like Earl.

The mice stayed out of the way of Farmer Bob and his wife Karen, who knew the mice were around but as long as they didn't mess things up Bob and Karen tolerated them. But for the life of them they couldn't figure out why Earl couldn't catch them darn mice.

Karen thought to herself Earl would catch those mice sooner or later. In the mean time the mice were checking on all the new babies being born and talking to the parents, that's why all the farm animals liked the three mice. The woodland animals like the mice to for the same reason. The mice would hang out in the woods on the side of the mountain behind the Barn that was about to fall down. That's where they would hear the bad cat Earl and his buddy's make plans to catch the mice or torment the smaller farm animals.

Tuesday morning started off like any other day, the mice were about to go off into the woods when they caught a glimpse of Earl and his buddies heading towards the rabbit family. The rabbits just had eight babies, Earl and his buddies were on their way to harass them. the cats thought they would practice their hunting skills on the rabbits.

Some how the mice had to get to the rabbits before the cats. Trickey came up with a idea to distract the cats by running across their path into a hole that one of their mice's friends had dug. This would give Slickey and Ickey time to warn the rabbits. When the cats got close enough Trickey took off running in front of them, he knew the cats were easily distracted so they gave chase, just when they thought they had him, Trickey dove into the hole. Those silly cats waited a while to see if Trickey was going to come back out. What they didn't know was the hole was a tunnel that came out underneath a log about 10 feet behind them. Trickey came out the other end and caught up with the other 2 mice. They high tailed it to the rabbits to warn them, but the rabbits were already gone. The mice wondered where the rabbits had gone. The mice heard a commotion not to far away and noticed a couple cats they had never seen before chasing the mom and dad rabbits. The mice looked for the babies, found them and led the babies to one of mice's favorite hiding places. These new cats didn't know there were babies, that's why the rabbit parents ran away from the nest.

This time Slickey had an idea, he finally caught up with the rabbits and told them to follow him. When they were alittle ahead of the new cats Slickey told the rabbits what he had in mind. So the mom and dad rabbit followed Slickey, in no time they led those new cats right to Earl and his buddies

who could not believe what they were seeing. those new cats had crossed the creek and were now on Earl's side of the creek. It didn't take Earl and his buddies long to forget all about the rabbits and the mice. They got very angry and had to take care of these new cats on their turf. The mice nor the rabbits wanted to stick around for what was about to happen.

That evening when Earl got home he was missing some fur and was not in a good mood. He ate his food that the farmers wife left for him, then he went to meet his buddies at their secret place. His friends were already there waiting on him. The mice followed Earl because they wanted to hear what the cats were up to. Earl's friends weren't happy either, they too had patches of fur missing. Earl started the conversation on how to get rid of these new cats on their turf. We got the best of them today but I heard one of them say they would bring their buddies next time and settle things. Earl told his buddies he wasn't going to give up his turf with all the farm animals, because they were outnumbered.We'll have to come up with something to make those other cats stay on their side of the creek. if they didn't the new cats would take over Earls turf and everything on it. That meant the mice and all the farm animals that Earl and his buddies loved to chase and torture. But Earl new these new cats would be 10 times worse than he and his friends were to the farm animals.

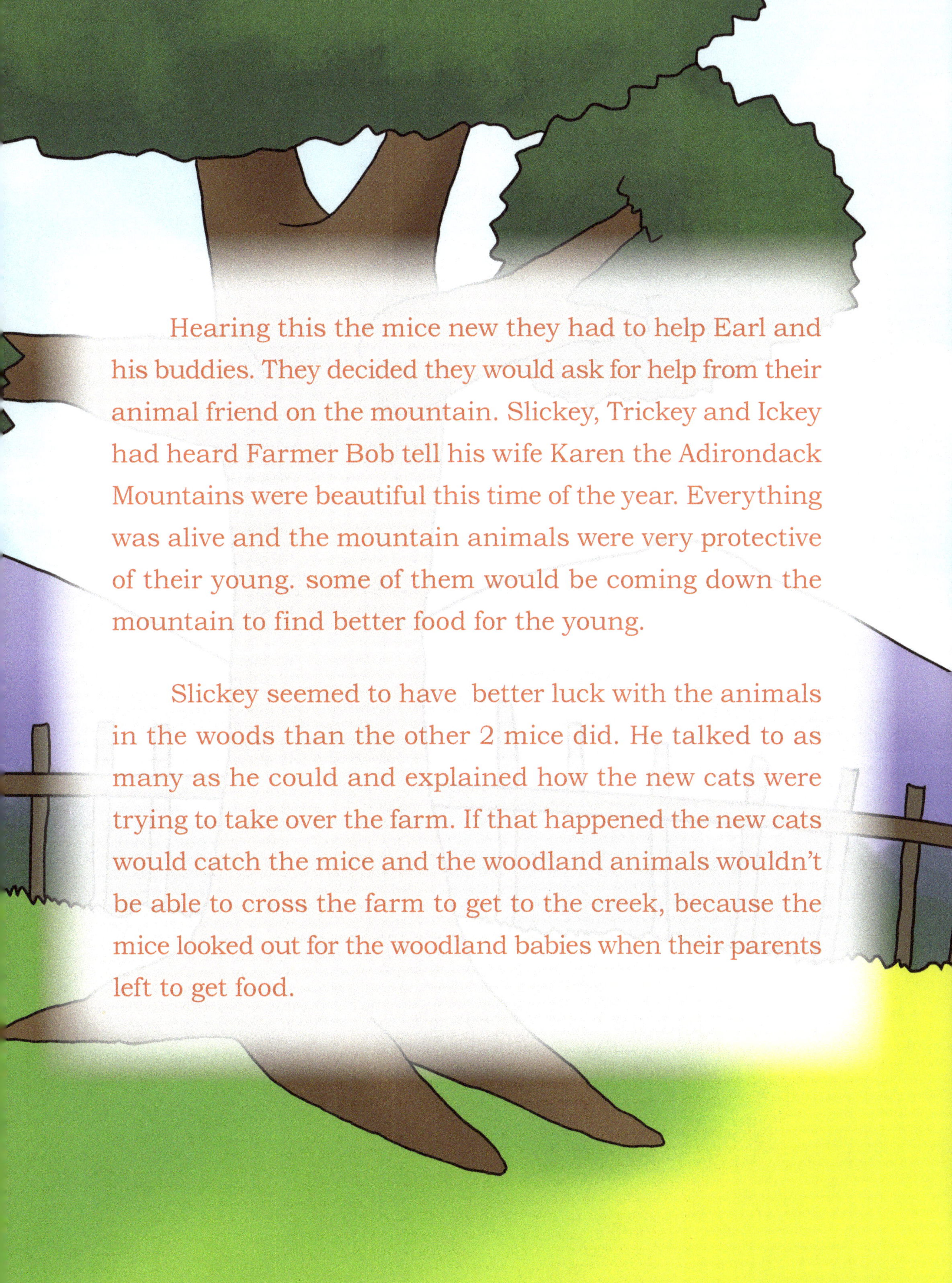

Hearing this the mice new they had to help Earl and his buddies. They decided they would ask for help from their animal friend on the mountain. Slickey, Trickey and Ickey had heard Farmer Bob tell his wife Karen the Adirondack Mountains were beautiful this time of the year. Everything was alive and the mountain animals were very protective of their young. some of them would be coming down the mountain to find better food for the young.

Slickey seemed to have better luck with the animals in the woods than the other 2 mice did. He talked to as many as he could and explained how the new cats were trying to take over the farm. If that happened the new cats would catch the mice and the woodland animals wouldn't be able to cross the farm to get to the creek, because the mice looked out for the woodland babies when their parents left to get food.

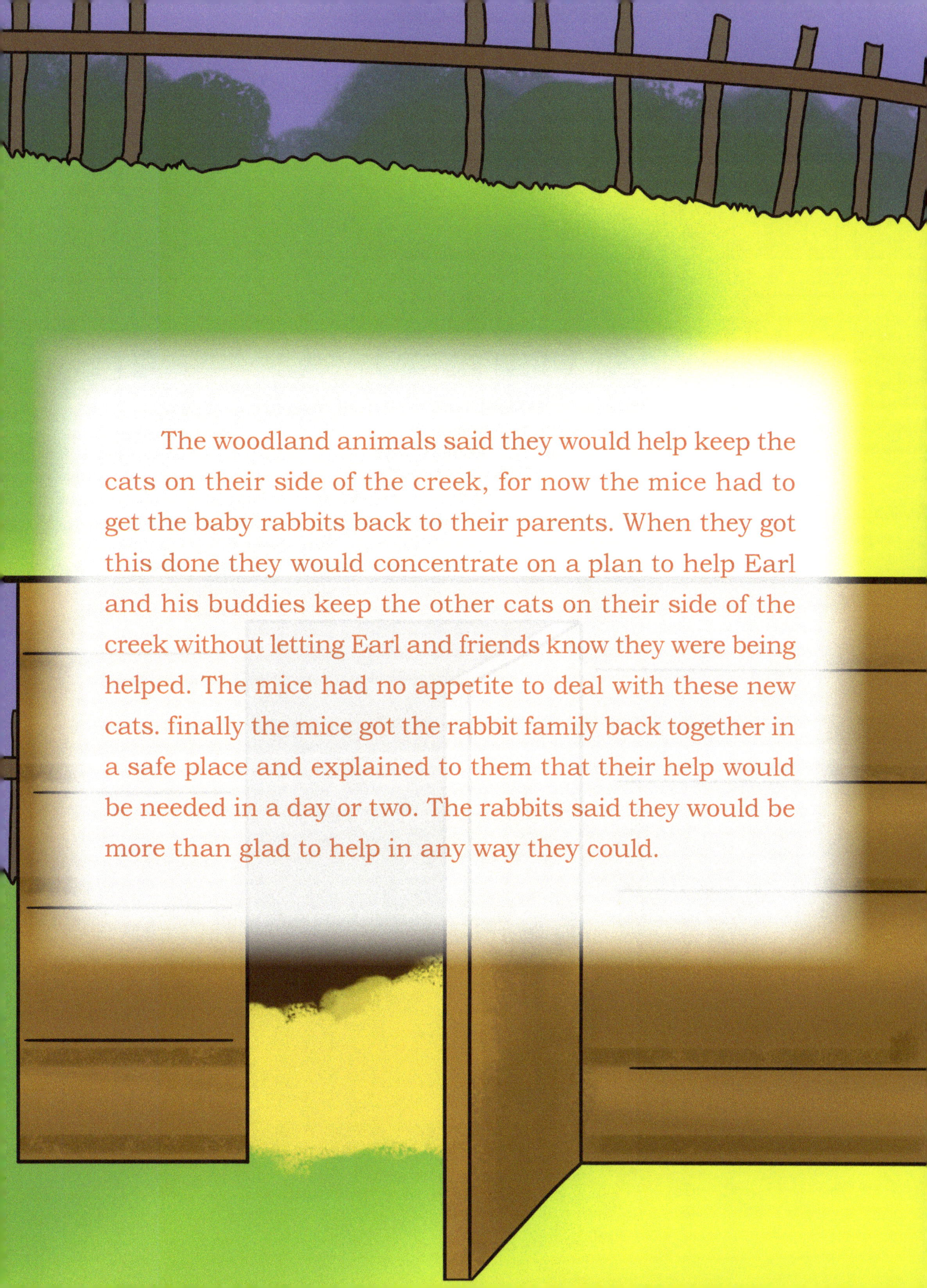

The woodland animals said they would help keep the cats on their side of the creek, for now the mice had to get the baby rabbits back to their parents. When they got this done they would concentrate on a plan to help Earl and his buddies keep the other cats on their side of the creek without letting Earl and friends know they were being helped. The mice had no appetite to deal with these new cats. finally the mice got the rabbit family back together in a safe place and explained to them that their help would be needed in a day or two. The rabbits said they would be more than glad to help in any way they could.

That afternoon the mice got everyone together to explain what they thought had to be done. it would be kinda tricky but that's why they called it tricky Trickey. Working together was always the best way to go. All this activity didn't go unnoticed by either group of cats. The cats were wondering why the mice kept running into the woods and staying most of the day, then come home acting like something big was up. The cats knew the mice had friends in the woods, but they never stayed all day before.

Earl got together with his friends to come up with a plan to get the other cats off their turf. Benny, Earl's best friend, came up with an idea to cross the creek late at night and destroy stuff on the other cats property. That way when that farmer saw all the damage the next morning he would blame those cats and get rid of them. This was the dumbest thing that could have came out of Benny's mouth but Earl and the rest of his buddies thought it was a great idea!

Meanwhile the mice, rabbits and woodland animals were almost ready to make their move. but first Trickey had to ask some of the field mice for their help too. That evening Earl and his crew crossed the creek on the old rotten log to the other cats home. Earl and his crew began turning over flower pots, digging in the flower beds and opened all the cages/gates to let the other animals out. Then they hid till the farmer came out later. They wanted to see what he would do to those other cats. Sure enough he was so upset he put those cats in some of the cages and said this was the last straw, the cats had to go. The farmer spent the day rounding up the loose animals, when he was on his way back to the house he saw the cats had escaped from the cages he put them in but didn't see them anywhere. He was glad, he thought they left on their on.

Those cats knew who did the damage and the wanted to get even with Earl and his buddies. The war was on, they wanted to show their farmer who the real culprits were. The rabbits and woodland animals were ready for Slickey, Trickey and Ickey to put their plan into action. They finally got started, all the friends in the woods started coming down the mountain, starting with the big animals, all the new babies were mixed in with the rest of the parents. The cats across the creek saw this first, then Earl and his buddies. They all wanted to get closer to see what was happening.

Once the woodland animals started to cross the creek the farmers started pulling up to make a path that the migrating animals could use to get to the other side of the highway to the meadows to graze and raise the young. The Native Americans used to burn the meadows to help it grow better and thicker but that was no longer possible for the farmers to do. The farmers asked the Native Americans what they could do to get the same results. The Native Americans said to let the wild animals graze the meadows to keep the grass low.

All the cats ended up on the same side of the creek so they started to put their plans in motion against each other. When out of nowhere rabbits and all kinds of small animals started running across the log to cross the creek and at that moment all the cats forgot about their fued and gave chase. in the meantime some of the big animals had made their way back to the creek unbeknown to the cats. The small animals circled back to the log just as the cats were about to catch up with them running behind the bigger animals. The cats had to jump in the creek to avoid the bigger animals and we know how cats hate to be in water. When they got to a place they felt safe they got out of the creek, they were too far away to start chasing the smaller animals again nor did they have any energy left. They knew they'd been tricked.

All the animals thanked each other for plotting against the cats. Their plan worked and hopefully all those cats learned a lesson. Of course The Bad Cat Earl and his buddies said they would get even with all of them. But that, That's another tail. The End!!!

10620 Treena Street, Suite 230
San Diego, California,
CA 92131 USA
www.readersmagnet.com
1.619.354.2643